Designed by Flowerpot Press
www.FlowerpotPress.com
DJS-0912-0176
ISBN: 978-1-4867-1464-3
Made in China/Fabriqué en Chine

COLORS

Written by

Jenna Kurtzweil

Illustrated by

David Rodriguez Lorenzo

When long ago the world was young and everything was new, there remained a certain something very special left to do.

For everything across the land was clear as clear could be,
from elephants and canyons to the dolphins and the sea.

It seemed the world was hardly there and so it was decided that Colors could improve it with the beauty they provided.

The Colors all agreed that they would love to lend a hand.
They were eager and excited for the chance to paint the land.

To Yellow went the mighty sun. To Orange went the flame.
Even lovely little Lilac won a flower with its name.

To Gold was given honey. To Silver went the moon.
Black and White agreed to share the panda and raccoon.

And higher still the open sky was chosen just for Blue.
And with it came the oceans, lakes and seas, and rivers, too.

Sturdy Brown became the soil, the trunks, and roots of trees, while Green loved climbing high to get the vines and lofty leaves.

Purple fancied grapes and plums. Red requested roses.

Pink flew on flamingos' wings and covered puppies' noses.

Gray the gentle giant claimed the mountain's rocky throne,
while Emerald and Ruby chose to dwell within the stone.

When every Color present thought the world a pleasant place,
they chose to leave some holes and gaps and bits of empty space.

Some things were left transparent and are see—through to this day,
like wind that rustles treetops or the words that people say.

And with the many Colors, big and bright and pale and small,
there still remains one special way to unify them all.

When rainy weather hides the sun and Colors seem to fade,
they're really just preparing for the masterpiece they've made.

For after every rainfall when the sun starts breaking through, a rainbow can appear like it's been painted just for you!

From the beauty of a field in spring to a winter cold and clear, each and every living thing will find its Color here.

And in the rainbow lies a message Colors love to share:
unity is beauty and we find our best selves there.

So embrace the world and all the Colors, all the shades and hues.
Each one can be your favorite. Colors won't ask you to choose.